Miss Bindergarten Gets Ready for Kindergarten

Miss Bindergarten

Gets Ready for Kindergarten

by **JOSEPH SLATE**

illustrated by **ASHLEY WOLFF**

SCHOLASTIC INC.
New York Toronto London Auckland Sydney

ISBN 0-590-63567-0

Text copyright © 1996 by Joseph Slate. Illustrations copyright © 1996 by Ashley Wolff. All rights reserved.
Published by Scholastic Inc., 555 Broadway, New York, NY 10012, by arrangement with Dutton Children's Books, a division of Penguin Putnam Inc.

SCHOLASTIC and associated logos are trademarks and/or registered trademarks of Scholastic Inc.

12 11 10 9 8 7 6 5 4 3 2   8 9/9 0 1 2 3/0

Printed in the U.S.A.   14

First Scholastic printing, September 1998

To Maureen Sheridan Johnson
and all the other Miss Bindergartens,
wherever you are —J.S.

For Margy and Bill,
two of my favorite teachers —A.W.

It is the first day
of kindergarten,
and—
oh, oh, oh!—

Adam Krupp
wakes up.

Brenda Heath brushes her teeth.

Christopher Beaker finds his sneaker.

Miss Bindergarten gets ready for kindergarten.

Danny Hess
rushes to dress.

Emily Moko
cools her cocoa.

Fran Lister
kisses her sister.

Miss Bindergarten gets ready for kindergarten.

Gwen McGunny
packs her bunny.

Henry Fetter
fights his sweater.

Ian Lowe says, "I won't go!"

Miss Bindergarten gets ready for kindergarten.

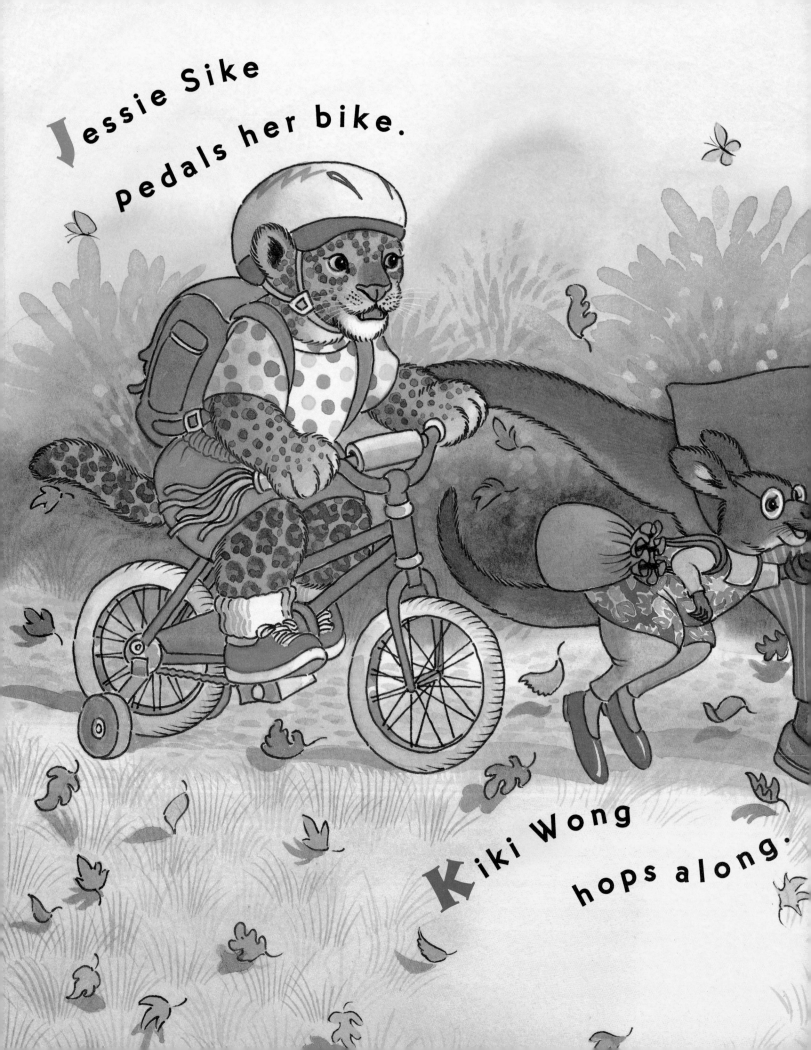

Jessie Sike pedals her bike.

Kiki Wong hops along.

Lenny Loome says, "Vroo-vroo-vrooom!"

Miss Bindergarten gets ready for kindergarten.

Matty Lindo looks out the window.

Ophelia Nye hugs good-bye.

Noah Bonn climbs right on.

WATCH YOUR STEP

Miss Bindergarten gets ready for kindergarten.

Patricia Packer
sneaks a cracker.

Quentin Wend
high-fives his friend.

Miss Bindergarten is *almost* ready

for kindergarten.

Tommy Tuttle
jumps a puddle.

Ursula Crewe

ties her shoe.

Vicky Densel

bites her pencil.

Now Miss Bindergarten is all ready

for kindergarten.

Wanda Chin
marches in.

Xavier Roe
yells
"Hello!"

Yolanda Pound looks around.

Zach Blair finds his chair.

"Good morning, kindergarten,"

says Miss Bindergarten.

And—oh, oh, oh!—

the fun's begun!

Adam · Alligator

Brenda · Beaver

Christopher · Cat

Danny · Dog

Emily · Elephant

Fran · Frog

Gwen · Gorilla

Henry · Hippopotamu

Ian · Iguana

Jessie · Jaguar

Kiki · Kangaroo

Lenny · Lion

Matty · Moose

Noah · Newt

Ophelia · Otter

Patricia · Pig

Quentin · Quokka

Raffie · Rhinoceros

Sara · Squirrel

Tommy · Tiger

Ursula · Uakari monkey

Vicki · Vole

Wanda · Wolf

Xavier · Xenosaurus

Yolanda · Yak

Zach · Zebra